© VANDRING
The Hedgehog Leaves Home
Text: Ulf Stark
Illustrations: Ann-Cathrine Sigrid Ståhlberg
Graphic design: Pierre Österholm
International editor: Janet Colletti, Boco Text Studio/Boco AB
North American adaptation: Boco Text Studio/Boco AB
Translation: Comactiva Translations AB, Sweden
Typesetting: Gyllene Snittet AB, Sweden
Project manager: Lena Allblom, IKEA FAMILY
Project co-ordinator: Anders Truedsson, TITEL Books AB
Produced by IKEA FAMILY
Paper: Arcoset
Printing: Litopat S.p.A, Italy 2011

Ulf Stark
Ann-Cathrine Sigrid Ståhlberg

The Hedgehog
Leaves Home

All of a sudden, fall arrived.

The leaves on the trees turned yellow and red. Mushrooms pushed up out of the ground. And it grew colder day by day.

"You are big enough to make your own way in the world now," said the hedgehog's mommy, giving him a kiss. "Just watch out for all the dangers in the big wide world."

"I will," said the hedgehog.

"And learn as much as you can."

"I will," said the hedgehog.

And off he set into the forest to find a place to sleep for the winter.

He was proud to be so grown up.

And he planned to learn as much as he could.

"The hedgehog is leaving home," said the ladybug from her spot on the rowan leaf.

"It is hard to believe that fall's already here," sang the mosquitoes in the bushes.

How strange they sound when they sing, thought the hedgehog.

Then he remembered what his mommy had told him: that he should watch out. But suddenly he stumbled and rolled down the hill like a ball.

Well, I have learned something now, he thought once he had come to a stop.

He had learned that rolling was fun.

At the bottom of the hill there was a pond. He looked into the water. There was another hedgehog there!

"Hello," he said. "Have you seen how grown up I am?"

Then the frog, who was sitting nearby, laughed.

"Are you talking to your own reflection?" she laughed.

The hedgehog felt silly.

"And I suppose you catch flies with your tongue!" he said quickly. "Do they taste good?"

"It's the most delicious food around," croaked the frog.

So the hedgehog stuck his tongue out too. But he didn't catch any flies.

"Goodbye, I'm going for a little dip," said the frog, and jumped in the pond.

"I'll join you," said the hedgehog cheerfully.

But he did not like it.

So he had learned two things: that he could not catch flies with his tongue, and he did not like swimming.

So off he went with wet paws.

Underneath some pine trees, beautiful mushrooms were growing. Red ones with white dots.

They look absolutely delicious, he thought.

He had already opened his mouth to take a bite when someone shouted:

"No! Not one of those. They're toadstool mushrooms, they're poisonous!"

A field mouse peeked out from behind a fern.

She was a kind mouse. Even though it had almost grown dark, she took the hedgehog to a place that had yellow mushrooms instead.

"These are chanterelle mushrooms. You can eat these," she said.

"What a lot I'm learning," said the hedgehog and took a big bite.

He was lucky as well, because there was a worm inside.

Hedgehogs like eating worms.

He was just finishing eating when he heard a swooshing sound in the air.

"Help!" squeaked the mouse. "Somebody wants me for dinner!"

The hedgehog remembered about watching out, so he looked up.

Oh my! What was that? It was a big owl diving down from the sky.
It looked at the mouse hungrily.

"Hide underneath me," said the hedgehog.

He lay over the mouse. At the last moment, the owl turned and flew away.
It did not want to get spines in its beak.

"Thank you kind hedgehog, you saved my life," said the mouse.

"And you saved mine before," said the hedgehog.

So he learned that it is always good to help others.

And sometimes, others help you.

The next day, the hedgehog continued his long journey.

The mouse kept him company for a while.

"Where are you going?" asked the mouse.

"Somewhere warm," said the hedgehog. "I am going to sleep for the whole winter. That's what my mommy said. Is that what you're going to do too?"

"No, not me. But the snakes and bears sleep all winter," said the mouse.

"You are so smart," said the hedgehog. "Can you teach me EVERYTHING please?"

"I don't have time," said the mouse. "But I can teach you some things."

So she taught the hedgehog what jackrabbit poop looks like.

"It might not be very useful information," she said. "But it's always fun to know."

After a while they saw a moose grazing on a shrub.

"Hello moose," called the mouse. "This is hedgehog. He hardly knows anything. I am showing him around the forest."

"That's very good," said the moose.

So the hedgehog and the mouse continued on their way and walked up a hill. Suddenly, a pine cone rolled right in front of them.

"The squirrel has been nibbling on this one," said the mouse. "He is a cousin of mine, we both have large front teeth."

She was interrupted by the squirrel calling from the branches above:

"Watch out, watch out, the fox is coming!"

Then they saw the fox. She was pointing at them with her tail.

"What do we have here?" the fox said to her cubs. "A mouse and a hedgehog. Let's hunt them. Just do what mommy does!"

And she took a great big leap.

Her cubs copied her. But they bumped into each other and rolled around laughing. And they got their tails all tangled together.

"Hurry up so they don't get away," said the fox.

"Hurry up so they don't catch us," said the mouse.

"I can't run very fast," said the hedgehog. "But I can roll."

The hedgehog rolled down the hill. Then he and the mouse crept into a hole.

When the fox tried to get in, she hurt her nose on the hedgehog's spines.

"Come on, let's go," said the fox to her cubs. "Hedgehogs don't taste very good anyway."

"Now I've learned two more things," said the hedgehog.

"What?" asked the mouse.

"That holes are good, and to watch out for foxes."

"You're right about that," said the mouse. "I have to go home now, see you in the spring!"

So the hedgehog and the mouse went their separate ways.

The hedgehog was getting more and more tired. He ate and drank.
And watched out for foxes.

But try as he might, he could not find a good place to sleep.

An ant was hurrying along the path, as fast as it could.

"Hello," said the hedgehog. "Where are you going to live this winter?"

"Under – puff, puff – my anthill, far below the ground," puffed the ant.

"Can I stay there too?"

"No – pant, pant – you are too big," said the ant and hurried on.

Soon the hedgehog heard somebody yawn.

It was a bear, stomping around the blueberry bushes picking berries.
She wanted to fill her tummy before she went to sleep for the winter.

"Aaaahhh, I'm so tired," she yawned.

"Watch out!" called the hedgehog.

The bear was just about to step on a poisonous snake.

"Sssss," hissed the snake. "I am going to bite this paw."

But before the snake could bite, the hedgehog was there. He held the snake by the neck. The snake whisked its tail around wildly, trying to get free.

Gosh, aren't I brave, thought the hedgehog. I did not know that before.

He was so surprised that his mouth gaped open.

The snake slipped away, and was gone, nowhere to be found.

"You saved me," said the bear. "What can I do for you?"

"I don't know," said the hedgehog. "I am looking for somewhere to sleep so that I can keep warm during the winter."

"You can sleep in my cave," said the bear.

The bear made a huge pile of leaves and twigs in her cave.

"There you go, my prickly friend," she said.

"Thank you bear," said the hedgehog, and crawled in.

It was nice and warm and cozy in there. The hedgehog felt very happy.
He had a nice place to sleep, and a nice friend to talk to.

He talked about the frog and the owl and the fox. He talked about
the mosquitoes and the ant. And about all the things he would do in the spring.

But the bear was already asleep.

And soon the hedgehog would be too. But first he thought: It is easier to be
out on your own when there are others there to help you.

And then he fell asleep.

Fox   Bear   Field mouse   Bird